Dad's Favorite Fish

WRITTEN AND ILLUSTRATED BY DUSTIN E. MURPHY

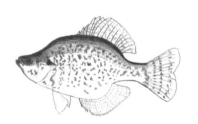
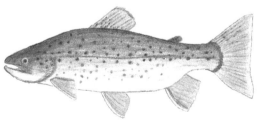
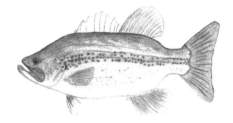

Dedicated to our three little fish:
Declan, Rowan, & Sawyer

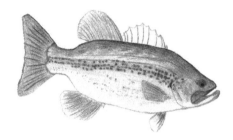
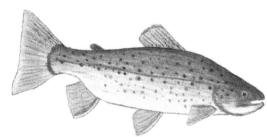
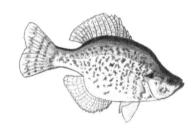

Published by Orange Hat Publishing 2021
ISBN 9781937165291

www.orangehatpublishing.com

Thank you to my amazing wife Lauren for all the love and support you have given me on our lifelong journey together. You truly are the catch of my life!

Dad's first favorite fish was Bluegill,

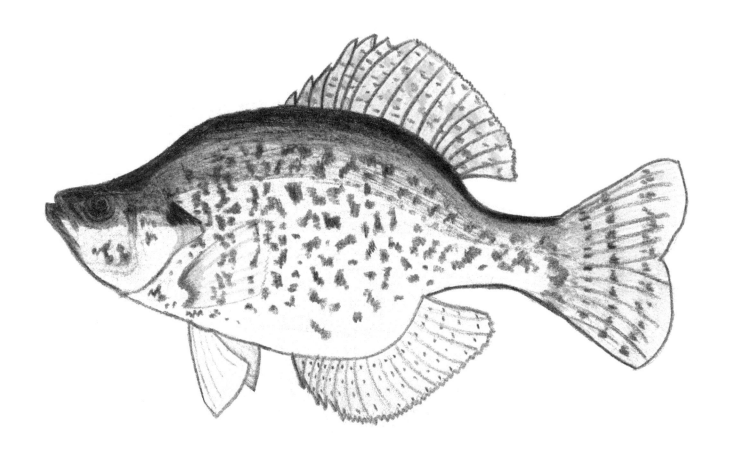

then Crappie.

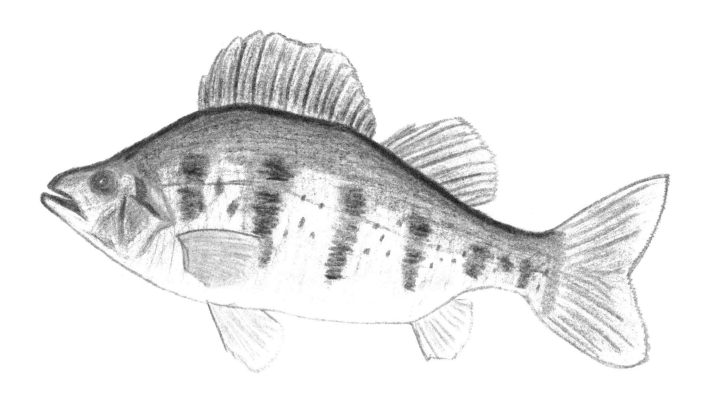

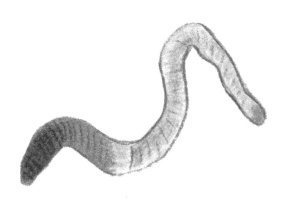

Followed by Perch,
with fingers still slimy.

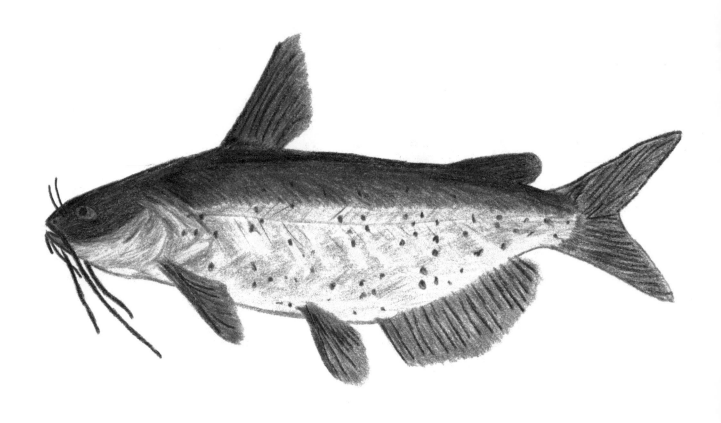

Then Catfish and Walleye were bigger.

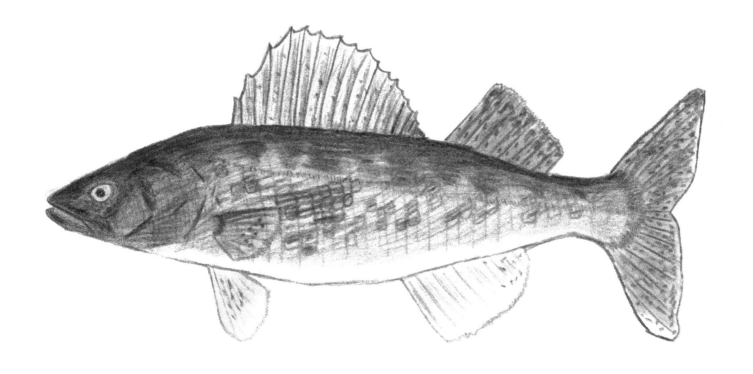

But messy.

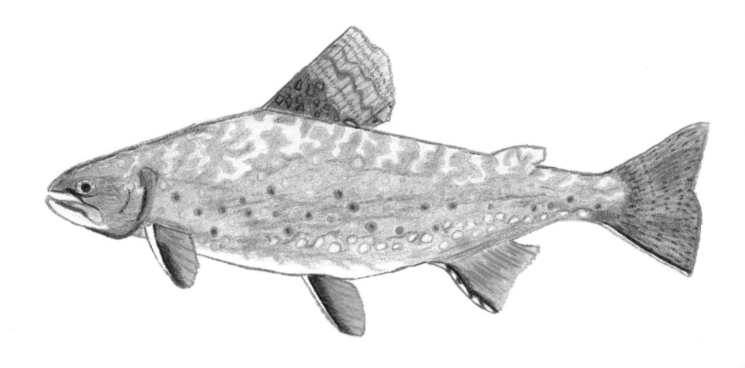

After Green

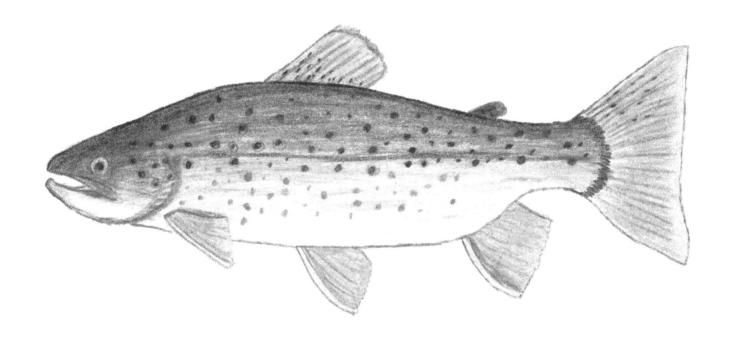

and Brown Trout,

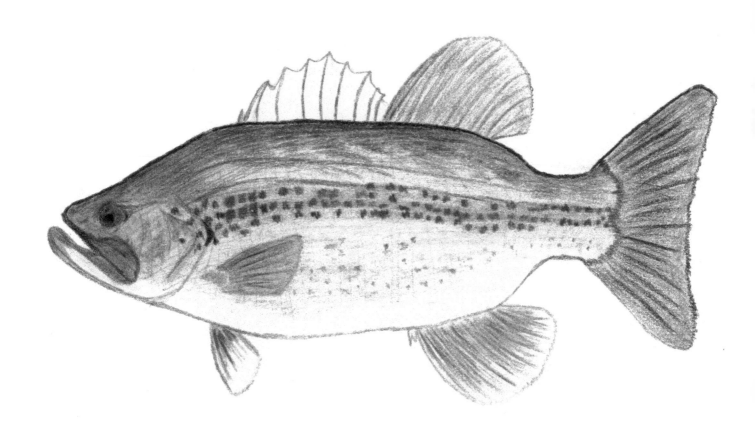

Dad caught Bass,

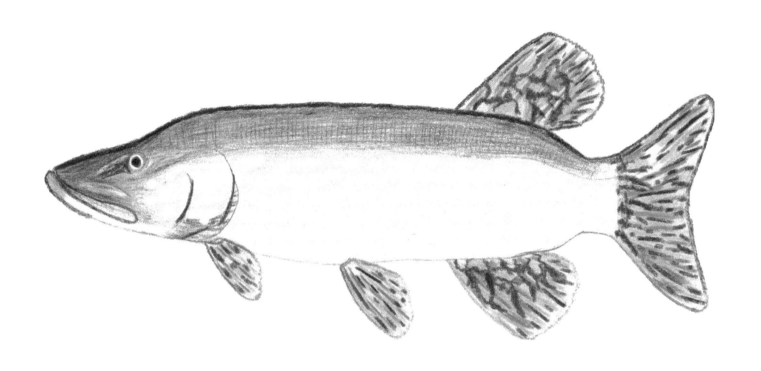

Pike,

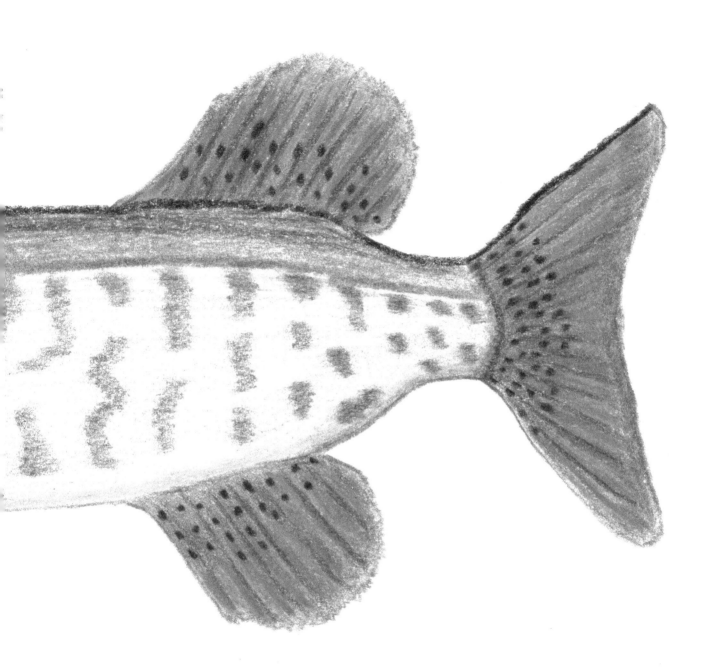

And Muskie!

Many memories of sunsets
And the boat trips we had.

But NO Fish compares
to being a Dad!

CPSIA information can be obtained
at www.ICGtesting.com
Printed in the USA
BVHW062247220821
614828BV00002B/21